DINOSAUR JUNIORS
Happy Hatchday

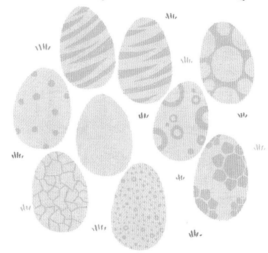

this book belongs to

```
..........................................
```

Once upon a long, long, long, long, long, long, long, long, long, long, long, long, long, long, long, long, long, long, long, long time ago...

For Greg, Helen, Noah and Sam

DINOSAUR JUNIORS
Happy Hatchday

Written and illustrated by

Rob Biddulph

HarperCollins *Children's Books*

First published in hardback in Great Britain by
HarperCollins Children's Books in 2018
First published in paperback in 2018

HarperCollins Children's Books is a division of HarperCollins Publishers Ltd.
Text and illustrations copyright © Rob Biddulph 2018
The author / illustrator asserts the moral right to be identified as the
author / illustrator of the work. A CIP catalogue record for this book
is available from the British Library. All rights reserved.

Visit our website at www.harpercollins.co.uk

ISBN: 978-0-00-820743-4
Printed and bound in China
1 3 5 7 9 10 8 6 4 2

FIVE THINGS TO FIND IN THIS BOOK
1. A pair of scissors ☐
2. A bottle of pop ☐
3. A silver trumpet ☐
4. A broken bar of chocolate ☐
5. A curious tortoise ☐

Nine perfect eggs.
A handsome batch.

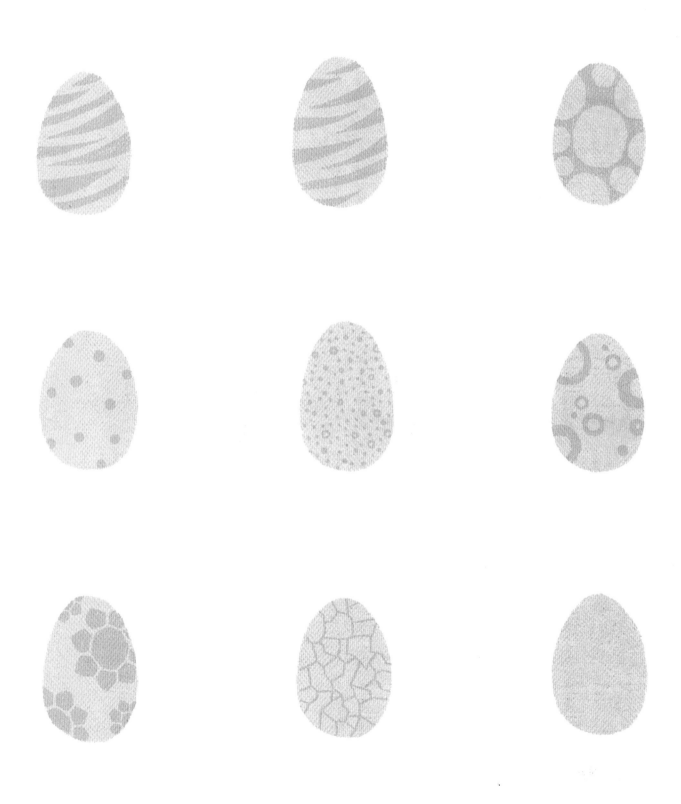

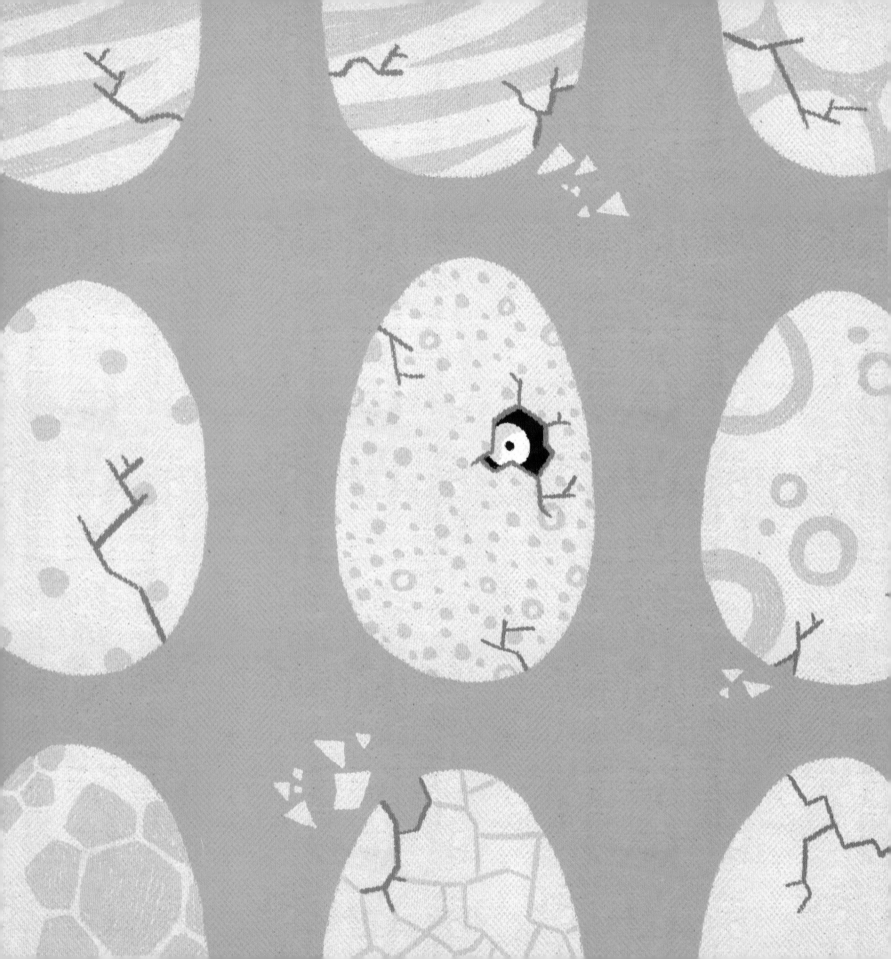

I spy an eye.

Let's watch them hatch...

Hi Otto,

Winnie,

Hector,

Sue.

Hi Nancy,

Martin,

Wilf

...AND I'M ZIGGY!

and Boo.

TAP
TAP

CRACK

But wait.
What's this?
One final egg.
A tap...
a crack...

"Hello. I'm Greg."*

Greg is short for *Gregosaurus*.
Makes it much less tricky for us.

The last of nine, Greg's really late.
A week behind the other eight.

So hurry up. No time to waste.
Go find some friends. More speed, less haste.

First up, it's Otto. Winnie too.
They're having fun with paint and glue.

"Oh dear," says Greg, "it's plain to see –
There's no room in their game for me."

What's this? Jam tarts? Eclairs? Ice cream?
It's Sue and Hector, chefs supreme.

"Oh dear," says Greg, "it's crystal clear –
These baking buds don't need me here."

Next up it's Nancy. Nice guitar.
And Martin's tuba – OOM-PAH-PAH!

"Oh dear," says Greg, "there is no doubt –
There's no way I could help them out."

One final stop. It's Wilf and Boo
And balloons! (I've counted twenty-two...)

Greg sighs beneath his thundercloud.
"Two's company, but three's a crowd."

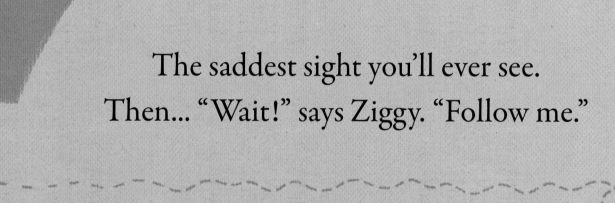

The saddest sight you'll ever see.
Then... "Wait!" says Ziggy. "Follow me."

THIS WAY

"Lift those spirits; dry those eyes. Get ready for a big...

Oh, Greg! This fab Cretaceous crew
Have planned a party just for you!

High fives,

fist bumps,

big hugs,

applause...

For disco-dancing dinosaurs!

Fin

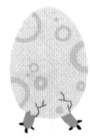